MW00958755

Does Melanie Like Melon?

Karin Gustafson

Copyright © 2016 Karin Gustafson (text and illustrations)

All rights reserved.

ISBN: 1541347579
ISBN-13: 978-1541347571

FOR MELANIE EDITH MARTIN

Does Melanie like melon?

Yes, she says, I do.

Cantaloupe and honeydew

and watermelon too.

Does Melanie like apples?

Yes, she says, I do.

Speckled red and shiny red;

green and yellow too.

Does Melanie like noodles?

Yes, she says, I do.

Sometimes with spaghetti sauce;

sometimes with tofu.

(Tofu?)

You know who else likes noodles?

Grant and Lacy-cat.

Sometimes for their dinner;

sometimes for a hat.

You know who else likes apples?

A horse named Mr. P.

He'll also eat a carrot

very happily.

Mr. P. eats melon

when the day is hot.

Sometimes the cats will sniff it;

sometimes they will not.

But Melanie likes melon best

with a friend or two.

Cantaloupe and water--

and sweet sweet honey dew.

ABOUT THE AUTHOR

Karin Gustafson lives with Grandpa Jay, right next door to Mr. P. Karin is terribly allergic to cats so can hardly even visit Grant and Lacy, but she has a lot of fun whenever she gets to see Melanie. Especially, when they eat melon.

Karin's other books are *1 Mississippi, Going on Somewhere, Nose Job, Nice* and *Dogspell.*

BackStroke

Books

Made in the USA
Middletown, DE
27 February 2022

61883605R00018